THE ADVENTURES OF SMELLY SOCK AND HIS FRIENDS INTO THE YARD

WRITTEN BY: RUSSELL DELK   ART BY: RYAN RADIS

To my wife,
May we always adventure.

Published by

BobbleHead Books, LLC

Laurel, MS 39440

Text Copyright @ 2018 by Russell Delk

All Illustrations Copyright @ 2018 by Ryan Radis

All rights reserved.

ISBN: 978-0-9987476-2-0

ISBN: 0998747629

Printed in the United States of America

Smelly Sock was so excited to go on his next adventure. He was eager to learn about his new friends and where they had come from. Each sock had a tale to tell.

Smelly Sock told of his battle with the velcro, while Chex talked about his unintentional tumble. Dot wound up getting stuck in the couch, and poor Wooly got left behind. Stripe's ordeal with static electricity was pretty scary, but not as bad as Argyle getting thrown in with the towels.

Well, at least we're safe in here." Dot said.
"That's true, but there's a time to play it safe, and a time for adventure. I say we go exploring!" Smelly Sock exclaimed.

The sock crew followed Smelly Sock into the hall. Noticing a bright light coming from a doorway, they all stepped in.

Once inside, they saw where the light was coming from. "What's up there?" asked Dot.
"Let's check it out!" Chex said.

The socks peered out the window and were amazed at what they saw. "What is this place?" asked Stripe.
"I believe it's called 'the yard,'" answered Smelly Sock.
"Well, what are we waiting for?! Let's go explore!"

"How do we get out there?" Wooly asked.
"We need to make a rope," Argyle replied. Tying bed
sheets together, they climbed out the window.

Out into the yard they went discovering new things around every corner. "What are you doing out here?" the lawn chair asked.

"Exploring," responded Smelly Sock. "Do you know of any cool things we can see?"

"I hear a lot of talk of a 'Fort' on the other side of the house. I would go there if I were you," the chair suggested. "But watch out for the owners dog Murry... he loves to chew on things."

"This Murry dog sounds kinda scary," trembled Dot.
"We better be extra careful."
"There it is!" Smelly Sock yelled as he found the fort.
"Oh, no! Look!" Wooly noted. "There's Murry dog!"

Sure enough, Murry was separating the sock crew from their destination.
"What are we going to do?" asked Stripe.
"We are going to reach the fort," declared Smelly Sock. "Come on guys, I have a plan."

"Your plans make me so nervous," quivered Dot.
"Besides, that Murry Dog is way too scary."
"Don't be afraid Dot," Smelly Sock said. "You're with friends, and we'll look out for you. Let's go ask that box on a wheel for help."

Approaching the wheel barrow, it woke up. "Hey, what are you doing out here? Shouldn't ya'll be inside?"

"We were inside, but we wanted to explore! Can you help us get to the fort on the other side of the house?" Smelly Sock asked.

"I'd love to help you but I have a flat, I can't roll. I bet if you go ask the lawnmower he could get you there. Go look for him in the shed."

"This place is scary." Dot said.
"Wow, look at all these things; they look sharp!"
added Wooly.
"Pay them no mind. As long as you're careful, they
won't harm you," came a voice from the dark corner.

"Who's there?" asked Smelly Sock.
"They call me the mower. The yard you just came from is where I work. What are you doing in here?"

"We're trying to get to the fort. Can you take us?"
asked Smelly Sock.
"Why do you need me?" the mower questioned.
"Well, we were headed that way when we saw the
Murry dog. We heard he's bad news and didn't want
to get chewed up," Smelly Sock explained.

"I see," said the mower. "Climb on board and let's go.
I feel confident I can get you there." They were
halfway to the fort when the noise from the mower
alerted Murry dog. Waking up, he spotted the sock
crew.

"Quick! Quick! Get us to the fort!" yelled the sock crew.

The mower tried its best to get to the fort, but it started to sputter. "I'm running out of gas! You'll have to make a run for it!"

The sock crew dashed to the fort and barely made it
before the Murry dog could reach them.
"Whew! That was a close one," Wooly said.

Into the fort they went and it was unlike anything they'd ever seen before. Suddenly a voice cried out, "Ahoy! Ye are a strange lot to be in here, aren't ye. What's your purpose for enterin' me abode?"

Smelly Sock spoke up, "We ventured out of the house to go exploring and wound up here."
"This is the Pirates' Cove Fort and Hang-Out Spot. Only the bravest venture out here," the pirate parrot said.

"I don't think I need to be here. I 'm not brave." Dot
muttered.
"Ye made it here to the Pirates' Cove Fort and Hang-
Out Spot, didn't ye? That means you're an explorer.
And explorers are brave," the pirate parrot explained.

"I never thought I could be Brave," said Dot.
"Aye, Matey, ye are a brave lass for sure. Here is a hat for the newest swashbuckler to join me crew." As the pirate parrot placed his hat on Dot's head, she beamed with bravery.
"Hey guys, look up here." Chex and Stripe said.

On top of the deck they could see the whole yard before them. Each sock took a turn looking through the telescope, and listening to the pirate parrot tell stories of past adventures.

With the sun setting, the sock crew realized it was time to head back home. "How are we going to get back to the house?" asked Argyle. "Murry dog is down there waiting on us."

"Perhaps I can be of assistance."

The sock crew turned to see a huge umbrella open.
"We would be so grateful if you could help us, but
how?" asked Wooly.
"The key is timing," the umbrella replied. "When the
wind hits me just right, I lift off and can fly all over the
yard."

"Hold on tight," the umbrella advised. "Get ready...
here comes the wind!" The umbrella flew off the fort,
headed to the house. Murry dog barked and jumped
to try and get the socks, but the umbrella was just out
of reach.

Coming to rest in front of the house, the sock crew were so grateful for the umbrella's ride.
"Oh you're quite welcome; I like to get out and explore myself sometimes, with the help of the wind of course," winked the umbrella.

Making sure they arrived safely, the pirate parrot spoke to Dot. "Keep a weather eye open, matey, and remember, always adventure." With that, the pirate parrot took off back to the Pirates' Cove Fort and Hang-Out Spot.

One by one, the socks helped each other through the mail slot on the front door. Making their way to the stairs, each sock recalled their favorite events from the day.

"Besides my new hat, I'd have to say exploring and discovering new things with my friends was my favorite part of the day," Dot said.

"I totally agree," replied Smelly Sock. "Adventures are fun, but adventures with friends are great."

"What a day!" shouted Smelly Sock.
Dot suddenly jumped on a box and addressed her crew mates, "Ahoy! I think you mean, what an adventure!"

If you enjoyed "The Adventures of Smelly Sock and his Friends -- Into the yard" be sure to check out these additional titles from Bobblehead Books!

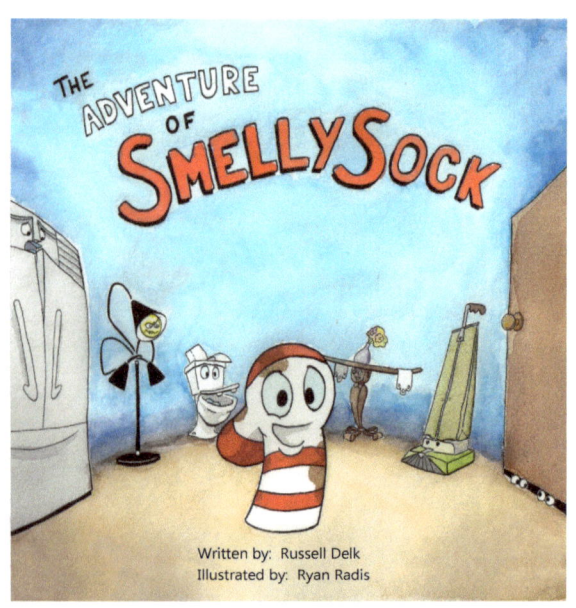

The Adventure of Smelly Sock

Sweet Mud